THERE WAS A ...
WHO SWA ...

5-MINUTE PHONICS

Short Vowel Sounds

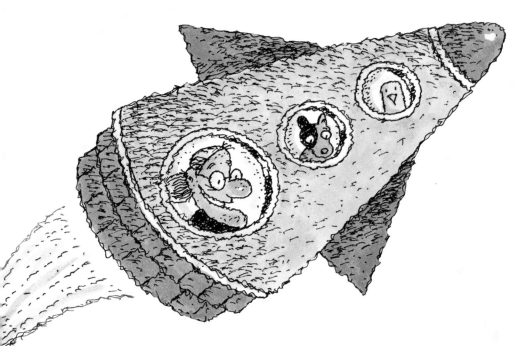

SCHOLASTIC INC.

Based on the Old Lady books by Lucille Colandro
Written by Quinlan B. Lee
Text © Lucille Colandro
Art copyright © 2025, 2017 by Jared D. Lee Studios

All rights reserved. Published by Scholastic Inc., *Publishers since 1920*. SCHOLASTIC and associated logos are trademarks and/or registered trademarks of Scholastic Inc.

The publisher does not have any control over and does not assume any responsibility for author or third-party websites or their content.

ISBN 978-1-5461-3812-9

10 9 8 7 6 5 4 3 2 1   25 26 27 28 29

Printed in the U.S.A.   40

This edition first printing, January 2025
Book design by Jennifer Rinaldi and David Neuhaus

TABLE OF CONTENTS

Introducing . . .

MAKE EVERY MINUTE COUNT!

GROWN-UPS: The stories and activities in this book feature short vowel sound and sight words. Here are some tips to help your early reader as they explore this book:

1. Read the story together.

2. Take turns sounding out the words.

3. Boost comprehension by asking questions about the text.

4. Have fun completing the activities together at the end of each story.

5. Revisit each story again and again to improve reading skills.

What do you think will happen next?

There Was an Old Lady Who Had a Fat Cat

This story features **short -a** words, which appear in bold type. Here are some to sound out while you read:

an	had	mat	snap
cat	lap	nap	that
fat	mad	rat	trap

There are also many must-know sight words in this story. Practice them to build reading fluency!

her	on	the	was
in	saw	there	who
not	she	to	

There was **an** old lady
who **had** a **fat cat**.
That cat liked to **nap**
in the old lady's **lap**.

Sleepy **cat**!

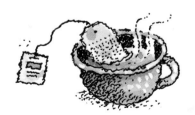

There was **an** old lady
who **had** a **fat cat**.
The **cat saw** a **rat**
run across the **mat**.

Look **at that, cat**!

There was **an** old lady
who **had** a **fat cat**.
The **cat** set a **trap**
while the old lady **napped**.

Clever **cat**!

There was **an** old lady
who **had** a **fat cat**.
The **cat** set a **trap**,
but the **trap** did not **snap**!

Lucky **rat**!

There was **an** old lady
who **had** a **fat cat**.
The **cat tapped** the **trap**.
The **fat cat** got **snapped**!

Poor **cat**!

There was **an** old lady
who woke from her **nap**.
She saw her **cat** in a **trap**.
She saw a **rat** on the **mat**.

Look **at that**!

There was **an** old lady
who just **had** to **laugh**.
She **laughed** **at** the **cat**
in the **trap**.
She **laughed** **at** the **rat**
on the **mat**.

She **laughed** like **mad**!

There was **an** old lady
who **had** a **fat cat**.
That cat just wanted to
nap in the old lady's **lap**.

In the story, the old lady's **cat** tries to catch a **rat** in a **trap**. **Cat**, **rat**, and **trap** are all **short -a** words. Look at the words below. They all have a **short -a** sound except one. Can you find it? Four of these words all rhyme with one another. What are the four words?

bat

lamp

cat

pup

hat

rat

map

apple

Answers on page 96

There Was an Old Lady Who Could Not Sleep in Her Bed

This story features **short -e** words, which appear in bold type. Here are some to sound out while you read:

bed	**kept**	**red**	**well**
best	**left**	**rest**	**wet**
fret	**mess**	**set**	**yet**
head	**pet**	**shell**	

There are also many must-know sight words in this story. Practice them to build reading fluency!

and	**did**	**it**	**this**
as	**had**	**not**	**was**
bad	**into**	**so**	**with**

There was an old lady
who could not sleep
in her **bed**.
She turned and she twisted
and covered her **head**.
Then she called to her dog,
"**Fred**, jump into this **bed**!"

There was an old lady
in **bed** with her dog.
She **slept** like a log,
in **bed** with her dog.
So she called her **pet** frog.

There was an old lady
in **bed** with two **pets**.
But she was not **set yet**,
in **bed** with two **pets**.
Her **next pet** was **wet**!

There was an old lady
who had birds in a **nest**.
But she thought it was **best**
if they **left** their small **nest**.
So she called **them** to come
into **bed** with the **rest**!

There was an old lady
with two furry **pets**.
They made quite a **mess**,
but she still did not **fret**.
She told **them** to come
into **bed** with the **rest**.

There was an old lady
who **kept** a crab in a **shell**.
It had a bad **smell**,
but it climbed in as **well**.

There was an old lady
with one more sleepyhead.
The other **pets** shook
when it **crept** near the **bed**.
"That is it!" she **yelled**,
with her face turning **red**.

There was an old lady
asleep in a **bed**.
It was cozy and warm, and
the **bed** said "**FRED**."

In the story, the old lady goes to bed, but she can't sleep. The word **bed** has a **short -e** sound. **Long -e** words are different—the **e** makes a sound like its name. The word **sleep** has a **long -e** sound.

Read the words below. Which words make the **short -e** sound and which make the **long -e** sound?

pen    **key**

shell    **jet**

bee    **egg**

bed    **queen**

Answers on page 96

There Was an Old Lady Who Took a Trip

This story features **short -i** words, which appear in bold type. Here are some to sound out while you read:

big	**fish**	**shrimp**	**tip**
dip	**in**	**sing**	**trip**
drink	**it**	**sip**	**wish**
fin	**ship**	**swim**	

There are also many must-know sight words in this story. Practice them to build reading fluency!

ate	new	saw	took
be	off	such	went
for	ran	that	when

There was an old lady
who took a **trip** on a **ship**.
The **ship** was so **big**!
This would be a fun **trip**.

There was an old lady
who took a **trip** on a **ship**.
She had fancy **drinks**
that she liked to **sip**.

There was an old lady
who took a **trip** on a **ship**.
She ate fancy **dinners**
of **squid**, **fish**, and **shrimp**.

There was an old lady
who took a **trip** on a **ship**.
She could **sing**.
She could **swing**.
It was such a great **trip**!

There was an old lady
who took a **dip** off the **ship**.
She went for a **swim**
and saw a **fin tip**!

There was an old lady
who had one last **wish**,
to **swim** for her life
when she saw that **big fish**!

There was an old lady
who ran off a **ship**.
She said she would never
again take that **trip**!

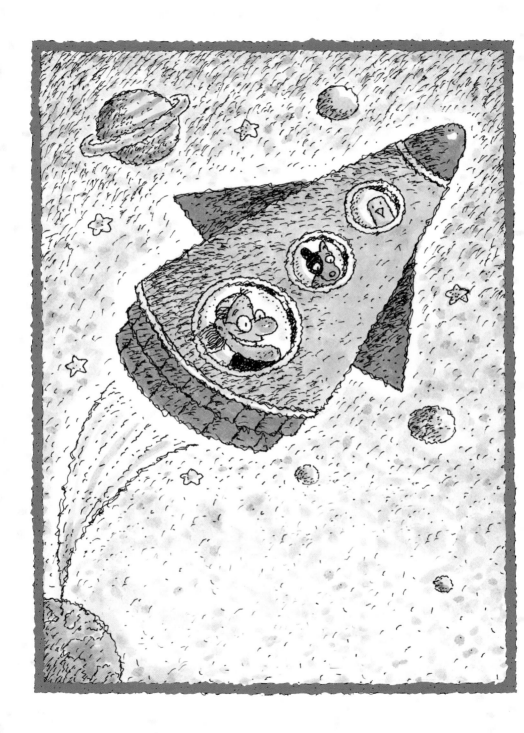

There was an old lady
who took a **trip**.
She flew off **in**
a new spaceship!

You read all about the old lady's **trip** on a **ship** in this story. The word **trip** has the same ending as **ship**. They both belong to the **-ip** word family. Other words in the **-ip** family are **skip** and **lip**.

Read the words below. Then make two new words for each word family!

fin   **_in** **_in**

chick   **_ick** **_ick**

fish  **_ish** **_ish**

dig  **_ig** **_ig**

kiss **_iss** **_iss**

Answers on page 96

There Was an Old Lady Who Went for a Jog

This story features **short -o** words, which appear in bold type. Here are some to sound out while you read:

blob	**hop**	**not**	**shop**
cob	**hot**	**off**	**stop**
flop	**jog**	**on**	
got	**log**	**pop**	

There are also many must-know sight words in this story. Practice them to build reading fluency!

and	**but**	**now**	**she**
ate	**like**	**old**	**want**
big	**made**	**out**	

There was an old lady
who ate corn **on** the **cob**,
cheese fries, and chili,
and a large shish kebab.

She felt like a **blob**.

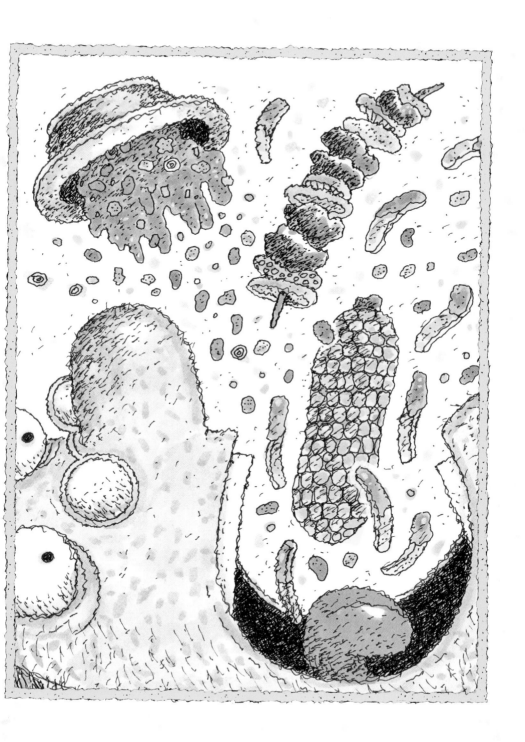

There was an old lady who went for a **jog**. She did **not** want to be a bump **on** a **log**.

So she went for a **jog**.

There was an old lady
who **got** very **hot**.
But she kept **jogging**,
even though she should **not**.

She was boiling **hot**!

There was an old lady
who did **not stop**.
So the corn in her belly
started to **pop**!

The **pop** made her **hop**!

There was an old lady
who had to **hop**.
She was so **hot** and tired,
she wanted to **stop**.

But she could **not**.

There was an old lady
who saw a sweet **shop**.
She had to cool **off**,
so she **popped** in the **shop**.

She still had to **hop**.

There was an old lady
who **got** an ice **pop**.
It cooled **off** her tummy.
She could finally **stop**.

She sat down with a **flop**.

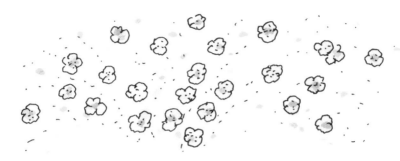

And with that big **flop**, out the corn **popped**. Now that store is a popcorn **shop**.

In the story, the old lady goes for a **jog**, but then she starts to **hop**. The words **jog** and **hop** have a **short -o** sound. **Long -o** words are different—the **o** makes a sound like its name. The word **old** has a **long -o** sound.

Read the words below. Which words make the **short -o** sound and which make the **long -o** sound?

frog

hot

boat

dog

rock

gold

hop

ghost

Answers on page 96

There Was an Old Lady Who Got Stuck

This story features **short -u** words, which appear in bold type. Here are some to sound out while you read:

buck	**fuss**	**skunk**	**truck**
bus	**luck**	**stuck**	**tub**
but	**muck**	**stunk**	**up**

There are also many must-know sight words in this story. Practice them to build reading fluency!

an	**good**	**it**	**so**
bad	**had**	**lot**	**some**
down	**her**	**of**	**when**

There was an old lady who rode on a **truck**. **But** the **truck** got **stuck** in a lot of **muck**.

There was an old lady
who was out of **luck**.
The **truck** was still **stuck**,
and she was covered
in **muck**!

There was an old lady
who had some good **luck**.
She **jumped** on a horse
and said, "Giddy-**up**!"

There was an old lady
who had some bad **luck**.
Her horse got mad.
It started to **buck**!

There was an old lady
who fell down near a **skunk**.
It **stuck up** its tail.
Psssst!
The old lady **stunk**!

There was an old lady
who **jumped** on a **bus**.
But when she got on,
there was a big **fuss**.

There was an old lady
who had some good **luck**.
The **bus** took her home.
She was still covered
in **muck**.

There was an old lady
who needed a **scrub**.
So she **jumped** in the **tub**.
Rub-a-**dub**-**dub**!

When the old lady's **truck** gets **stuck**, she has to find another way home! The word **truck** has the same ending as **stuck**. They both belong to the **-uck** word family. Other words in the **-uck** family are **duck** and **luck**.

Read the words below. Then make two new words for each word family!

mug **_ug** **_ug**

tub  **_ub** **_ub**

sun  **_un** **_un**

lunch  **_unch** **_unch**

skunk  **_unk** **_unk**

Answers on page 96

READING SKILL-BUILDERS

READING COMPREHENSION

 In *There Was an Old Lady Who Had a Fat Cat*, what did the cat see run across the mat? How did the cat try to catch it?

 There are lots of animals in the old lady's bed in the second story. Which animal smelled bad? Where did the old lady fall asleep at the end?

 Reread *There Was an Old Lady Who Took a Trip*. What are some things the old lady did on the ship? What did she see when she went swimming?

 What are some things the old lady ate in *There Was an Old Lady Who Went for a Jog*? What happened to her in the sweet shop?

 How did the old lady get stuck in the last story? What did she need when she finally got home?

VOCABULARY BOOSTERS

Sometimes, two words can mean almost the same thing. Knowing different words for the same thing is an important reading and writing skill. Look at the pictures below and read the words. Can you think of any other words that mean almost the same thing?

 bug
insect

 pup
dog

 hat
cap

 gift
present

Page 22

The word that does not have a **short -a** sound is **pup**.
The rhyming words are **bat**, **cat**, **hat**, and **rat.**

Page 40

Short -e words: pen, shell, jet, egg, bed
Long -e words: key, bee, queen

Page 58

Some suggested answers:
_in: pin, tin, bin
_ick: sick, kick, lick
_ish: dish, wish, swish
_ig: pig, wig, fig
_iss: hiss, miss, bliss

Can you think of any funny made-up words?

Page 76

Short -o words: frog, hot, dog, rock, hop
Long -o words: boat, gold, ghost

Page 94

Some suggested answers:
_ug: dug, hug, rug
_ub: rub, cub, sub
_un: bun, fun, run
_unch: bunch, crunch, punch
_unk: bunk, sunk, trunk